Lisa Marie

Mama's
words of wisdom

A sleepy homespun
lullaby from one
adoring mama to her son

Written By Lisa Marie Gilbert
Illustrated By Lorraine Shulba

Mama's Words of Wisdom by Lisa Gilbert. Published by Get You Visible Publishing. www.getyouvisible.com
Illustrations Copyright Lorraine Shulba

Special thanks to Tammy Schaetzle for her first illustrations of this story.

Heaven sent me an angel
with hellion tendencies

To my Rayne-bow:
Thank you for helping me find the sun.
You will always be the color in my sky.
Love Mama ox

When you look at me
with those baby blues,
on my heart strings you tug.

My Sweetlet, my Darling,
my Angel Snugglebug.

My favorite time of day
Is when we sing, laugh and play.
Dancin' and rockin', guitars in hand,.
Improv and giggles are parts of our band!

Work hard and play hard,
Fill your life with song.
Rock and roll saved your mama's soul.
Groove to your own beat and you can't go wrong.

A full life with laughter and love
Is what I wish for you.
Remember to never lose yourself;
Always stay pure and true.

Be a poet, a fireman, or a dad.
No matter which path you choose,
I will cheer you on.
I'm behind you win or lose.

When I'm feeling lost,
you help me find the light.
The color in my sky you are.

My rainbow, my sunshine,
My brilliant shooting star.

Always tell the truth,
It will set you free.
Your handshake is your word and bond.
Earning trust is your responsibility.

It is good to admit when you're wrong,
Your pride will still be there.
Your mama always has your back.
Learn from mistakes, be kind and fair.

When you find yourself in a struggle,
Forgive and forget are words to live by.
What goes around comes around.
Letting it go is more for you than the other guy.

If a friend lets you down
Never give up on what is right.
Be patient, confident, and use your words.
Pick your battles and your fight.

As you ride the rollercoaster of life,
The twists and turns, low and high.

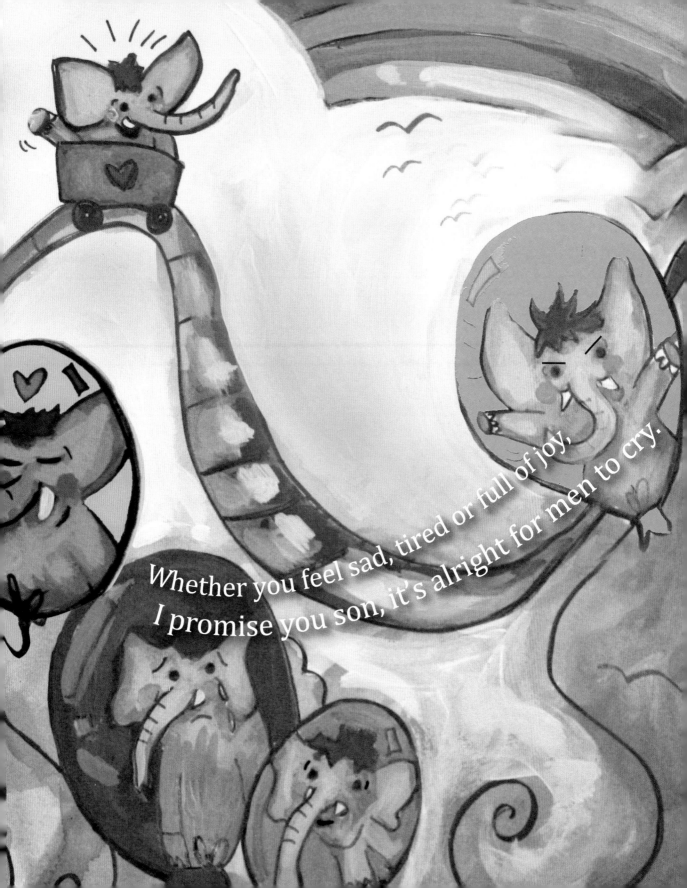

Whether you feel sad, tired or full of joy,
I promise you son, it's alright for men to cry.

Continue to be mindful and thoughtful,
Not afraid to speak your mind.
Listen with your heart
To become a man who is truly kind.

Always stand up for yourself and others
Against bullies, grinches and the like.
There is no place for name-calling or fists
So tell those meanies to take a hike!

What would Jesus do?
This is the path to follow.
The Father, Son and the Holy Ghost.
They are in your heart and should matter most.

The light of the holy spirit fills you up.
Say your prayers before you eat and sleep.
Remember others and give thanks
To fulfill the promise from God that's yours to keep.

You are the sun bursting through the clouds
Bringing joy and laughter with every touch and word.
A risk-taker, prankster and a clown,
You are unique and special, my little free bird.

Have courage and be brave,
Never let the beauty pass you by.
Take risks and follow your dreams,
I know you will soar high.

For my proud and fearless son

A final wish for you before I "make a mile" -

No matter what each day brings to you,
Always start and end your day
With a smile!

You are my greatest adventure
I was born to be your Mama
I love you with all my heart and soul

You will climb mountains, my boy.
Live with honor and grace

be a
☮RA NBOW✌
in someone else's cloud

This book belongs to:

I am   years Old.

I like reading this book with: